DEDICATION:

For all and any who hold a basketball try to dribble
and shoot and play practice on driveway cement
in Milwaukee Wisconsin streets practice bounce
p a s s e s on Harlem s c h oo ly a r d asphalt.

For all and any Ohio boys too small to get rebounds
girls who p u s h the two hand shots to the net
under California blue sky trees or in the s h a d e
of tallest buildings on g r a y s k y afternoons.

For all and any teachers out on playgrounds coaches
a l o n g the sidel i n e s older and o l de s t
friends and relatives and a l l i e s who justlove
and play and play along a n d make sandwiches.

For all and any daughter on the foul line
brother on the b e n c h
t e a m of p l a y e r s
g r o w i n g
t a l l
w i t h
j o y.

THE BASKET COUNTS

By **ARNOLD ADOFF**

Illustrated by **MICHAEL WEAVER**

SIMON & SCHUSTER BOOKS FOR YOUNG READERS

WE START WITH EARLY MORNING:

even before   the school bus,
as the sun just   shows   itself
east over the roofs
of the neighborhood. I am on
                    the drive,
                    p e bb le
                    r u bb er
                    b a l l
                    p o pping
                    u p into
                    m y right
                    p a l m,
onto the flattened
tips of five fingers. My   shot
is sweet as jelly on the toast.

On the bus my books are in the
b a c k p a c k on the floor.

The ball   is always   in my hand.

THE HOOP   BEHIND
THE BEDROOM DOOR:

Any soft small
       r o u n d
       fuzzy ball   **that fits the hand**
                          w i l l   f e e d
                          t h e   g a m e.

   Wadded paper
  very b a b y
stuffed bears
d o l l   heads:
a n y m a k e
b e l i e v e
       thing   **w i l l   f e e l**
                          t h e   s a m e
                          a s   o u t s i d e
                          d r i v i n g
                          t o   t h e h o o p.

I n s i d e   m y o w n   room
a f t e r   dinner, on raining
Saturday mornings, or   j u s t
because of ice or snow
I can always bounce fake turn r e a c h
              j u m p   s h o o t   s c o r e.
I can always d u n k s l a m d u n k

      behind   **the bedroom door.**

CITY SPRING:

Early   on   Saturday
            morning
        i n
M a r c h   I can
                    hear
                    the
        a l m o s t
        s i g h i n g
        of
        the   linking
play
ground
chain
link
fence   and
            the
soft
clang
b a n g i n g   o f
            r u s t y
                chains
                that
                hang
                from
        h   o   o   p   s.

WHEN MY FRIEND
WALTER SAYS:

we are going to play some
                              b a l l
he
is
not   ever   talking   about
any   horse   hair
        hard   ball   with
                    frankenstein
                s t i t c h e s.

Don't even think aboutping
                        p   o   n   g
football   soccer   kicks
or   c u r v e ball   pitches.

There is only one b a l l.
There is only one game.
There is only oneround
                    brown
                    ball
                through
                    one
                    steel
                    hoop.

IT IS THE FEEL OF THE PEBBLE RUBBER BALL:

on fingers

on p a l m

on fingers palm again whole hand

                                    hand

                                    hand

b o u n c e to b o u n c e

            to b o u n c e

            by h o u r s   and

                                    days

                                    and

                                    weeks

                                    and

                                    months

                                    and

                                    months

so   the   muscles

remember moves and my   eyes can finally

            look up and up and upand

            all around   as I make my

            way   down   the   court.

THE BASKET COUNTS:

ONE:

boy
  on foul line
bounces   ball
  to feel the
      p e b b l e
      r u b b e r
on finger tips
on   p a l m s
of   h a n d s.

Then ball to chest to push with force of toes
        to shoulders to arms to s h o o t:
    ball rises high in a rainbow arc until
    it
    falls
    into
    nothing
      but

      get

      the
      single
o n e   point
      score.

THE BASKET COUNTS:

TWO:

points for my team
as
I d r i b b l e
   d r i b b l e
   d r i b b l e
                    slide
                       to
                     just
                     this
                     side
of his
   a r m
   a n d
h a n d
   a n d
h e a d
   a n d I s h o o t
                   m y
               s h o t
               f r o m
               t h a t
           s w e e t
               s p o t
               j u s t
               n e a r
e n o u g h
            for
two
points for my team.

THE BASKET COUNTS:

THREE:

minutes as I move a r o u n d her moving body,
then set my feet and r a i s e my arms.
Her chopping arm and hand and hopping
hip all knock me a l m o s t to the floor.
But my shot flies up then down through net.

I love to hear the whistle sound sharp.
I love to watch the referee's right arm
and fingers chop down hard
and p o i n t to s i g n a l
s c o r e plus m o r e.
I love to make the f r e e throw sure
shot foul line: one and two
i s
always
three.

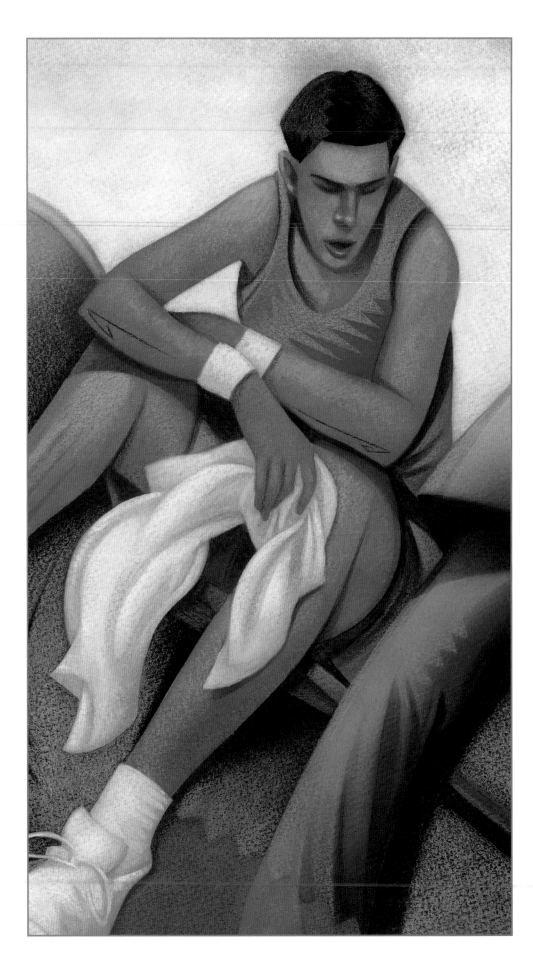

THE BASKET COUNTS:

FOUR:

s h o r t
quarters and four po ints b e h i n d
         and four missed s h o t s
              four
              foul shots   falling short.

              Four fumbled e a s y passes.
              Four fi n g e r s thickasthumbs.

When the whistle blows   I   just can't count
the number of words out of thec o a c h ' s
                                        mouth
              as I crawl on all fours
              to my place at the very
              end of the team bench.

THE BASKET COUNTS:

FIVE:

fingers on e a c h
                hand
                and
I can count
a l l   t h e
p l a y e r s
on the   c o u r t. Ten divided by two teams
                        equals   five   on my side
                        plus me   on the faredge
                                of the far end
                                of the   bench
                        equals s i x
                        minus o n e
                        equals f i v e
                        equals f i v e
                                only
                                five.
W i t h
f i v e
fingers of o n e
            h a n d
f i v e
players s t a n d
in circle together. T h e y are my t e a m.

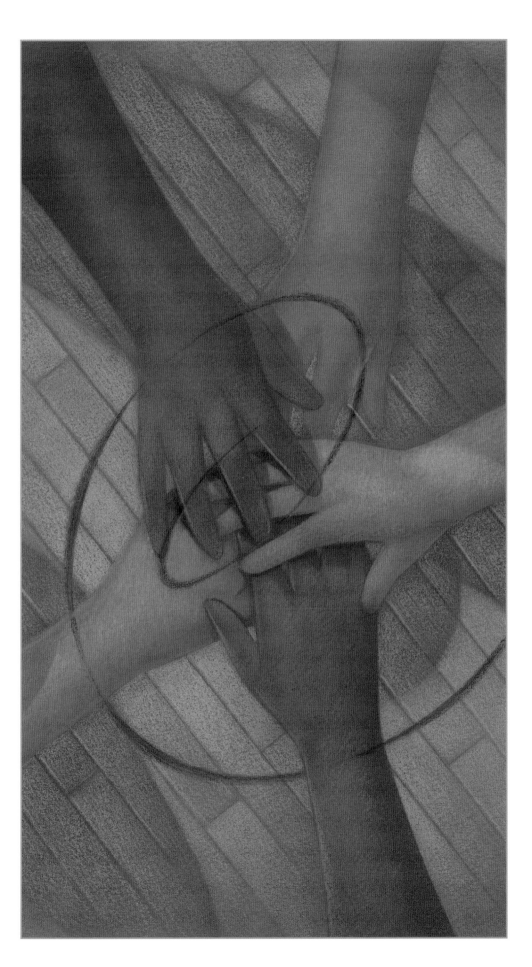

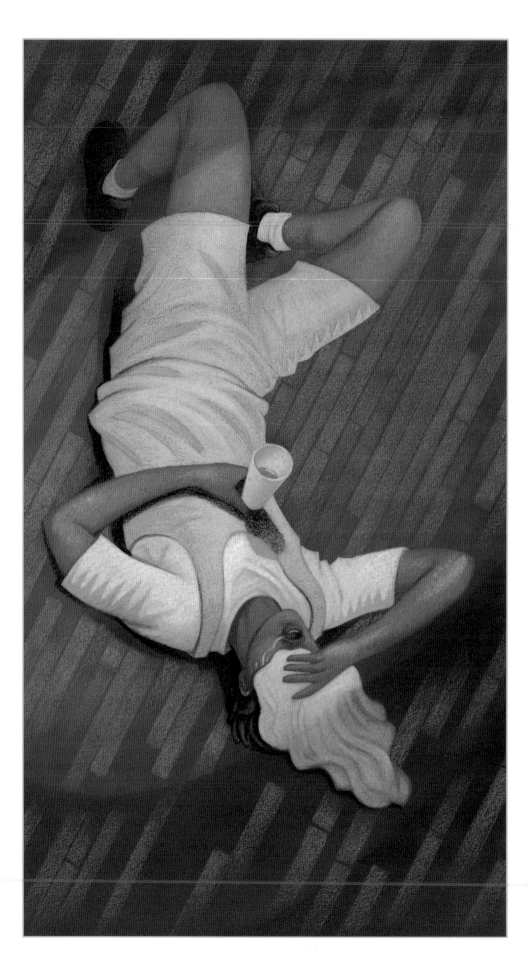

HALF
TIME:

I
lie
o n
the
flo or
almost
breathing
like
any
nor mal
m a l e
wha l e
a s
j u i c e
d r i p s
    o u t
        m y
m o u t h.

She
grips t h e wide
                drip
            mop, ready
            f o r
            t h e next
                    f a l l
            t h e
            ref's c a l l.
She
passes the towels,
            the   cups
                        of
            g r e   e n
            w a t   e r
              in
                to b i g
                    hands .
She
piles p a n t s
      j a c k e t s
        b e s i d e
                    t h e
                    b e n c h;
s l a m d u n k s
            j u n k
i n t o   baskets.

J

UMPER:

She

has

springs   in

k n ees and

f l i p

w r is t

f i n g e r

t i p s.

   Her

   shot

   arcs

s i lent ly

  through

  o p e n

  s t eel

   and

  c l ing

   ing

   net.

THIS

SHORT

G I R L:

with

long

colt

legs

d r i bb les

around   my

out

stretched

hands

and

legs for the

cl e an

l a y

u p

and

leaves

me

on

my

b a c k,

my

b u t t.

B a b y

sis ter.

BIG SISTER:

S h e   can run fast
    d r i b b l e
    to the right
      then pass
    to the   left.
S h e
    c a n   s i n k
    b a s k e t s
    like rocks in
    the   river.
S h e
    can win with
    cool bounce
    foul   shots
    f a ll i n g
    through net.
S h e
    can   think
    f a s t past
    the p l a y.
    We
    a ll
   y e ll
    her n a m e.
    W e   affirm
    her
    achieve ment
    her
    realiza t i o n
    of

    g   a   m   e.

BIG GIRL MUST
HAVE MOVED:

out   of   the   far   North   Woods
        or   some   Mid   West   f a r m
        or   some   m o u n t a i n
                                cabin
        or   s o m e   neighborhood
near
        that C l e v e l a n d lake
        that Chi c a g o   r i v e r.

She
has iron beam s h o u l d e r s
        elbows of razor s t e e l
even a forehead of r u s t red
                        c h u n k
                        m e t a l
                        h u n k s
all smashing my East
                Coast
                N e w
                Y o r k   thin
                                slim
                                body
into the very   h a r d
            w o o d f l o o r.

TARGET:

He is le a n i n g over,
his hands p u ll ing
                    down
on   the bottoms
of h i s u n i f o r m
                s h o r t s.

You can tell he is so
t i r e d, that eyes
                and hands
                and f e e t
will be
j u s t
t h a t
   extra
s l o w.

   Just
enough.

ALWAYS AND STILL THE LITTLE GUY:

I
bring
the
ball
down the court s m i l i n g
            a l m o s t
            t o o
            c a s u a l
            for a game.
Always
the
same: my grin brings your t w o
        big feet too close and I
                            a m
        past y o u r arms
        and in for the shot
        before you can turn.

                M e
                h o t .
                You
                burn.

IN YOUR FACE:

I
want
 you
  to
   recognize
            ize
            ize
   to
   memo rize
           ize
           ize

            the
            back
             of
             my
            head.

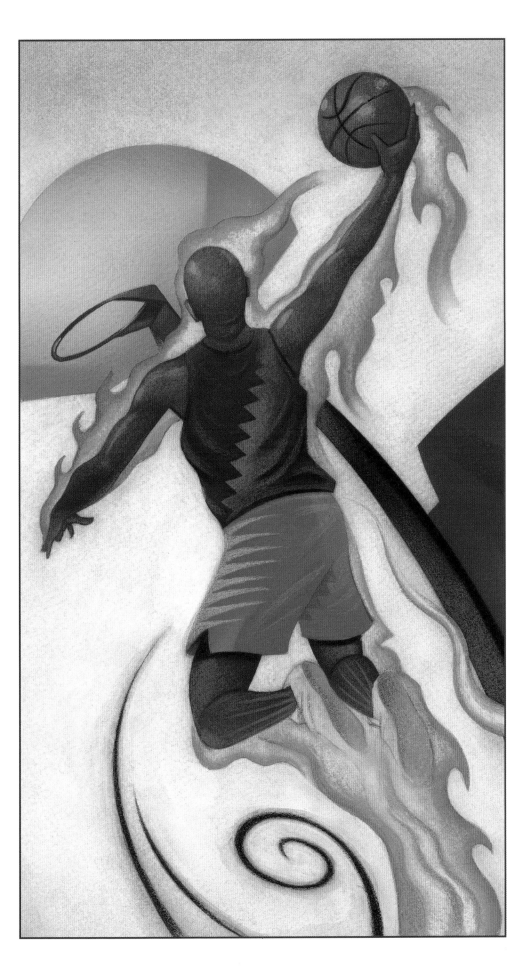

HIGH
FIVE:

1. Strap a jet propulsion pack on my back.
2. Find me some g i a n t w i n g s.
3. The Supreme (basketball) C o u r t
                              r e p e a l s
   The Law of G r a v i t y.
4. A very large
   ha nd reaches down through the roof
   of the school and holds me in two
                              t i g h t
                              f i n g e r s
   as I rise and walk on air   o v e r
                              e v e r y
                              h e a d.

5. I close my eyes   above the rim.
              and   lunch
                    e a t my

LUCKY SEVEN WISH LIST:

1. Give me l o n g   legs.
2. Give me l o n g e r arms and sharp elbows.
3. Give me l o n g e s t p   o   w   e   r fingers.
4. Give me l o n g   flap shorts

         and l o n g e r flip braids

         and s w e e t   g l i d e s

         and l o n g e s t   back

                      hand

                  passes.

5. Give me the a l l e y in the alleyoop play.

         and let me look one way and pass another.
6. Give me the dunk of my slamjam b r o t h e r.
7. Just

    Give me the dunk.

TEN TO LEARN:

1. Tie laces tight knot two times   then tuck in ends.
2. Pull shorts past hip bones for the hiphop look.
3. First shirt must have that Lisa Lovely number.
4. Killer curls are banded back a w a y from eyes.
5. Squeeze just right   and   water shoots in perfect

    a r c

    from water bottle i n t o o p e n mouth.
6. Dr i b b l e   to right look to left pass toright.
7. When to pass when to pass when to pass toshooter.
8. D o n o t smile at friends on o t h e r teams.
9. Think and plan ahead   and move and move and move.
10. H a v e a l l t h e s w e a t y w e t f u n.

PERSONAL   BEST:

In the end   the ball slides in   down the hoop
         or   the ball p o ps out. Re me m b e r:
the
trophy   is just some
                  hunk
         of   plastic
         just some
                  tin.

In the end you w   o   r   k as hard as you can.
Each time just jump   hands in air then flip
                        hands down for the fly
                                          ing
                                          ball.

Each   practice
a n d
each g a m e
a r e the sum
from the same
a dd it io n.

Personal best.

THIS TEAM THE SILVER SPOKES:

can   spin   and   fly   and   clutch

and   double

clutch

and

pop the s h a r p e s t wheelchair

wheeeelies   as

they

d r i b b l e pass c a t c h and

d r i v e on r o ll i n g   d o w n

the floor

to block and pass and sh oo t and score.

I need to make that happen

on my m o v i n g feet.

HOME GAMES:

Three   afternoons
               e a c h
               week
               some
               k i d s
               fro m
               t h i s
shelter down
the b l o c k come
               o v e r
                   to
               p l a y
               some
               b a l l.
We are all
on the same
               team.

OH LET ME FLY LIKE MICHAEL:

over
  the s t r e t c h i n g hands
  and a r m s and w i d e
                     b o d i e s
of   d e f e n s e w a l l s
  all
taller than World Trade towers.

I drink my milk   and take   double vitamins
and jog the sidewalks home each afternoon.
On the bed each night I s   t   r   e   t   c   h
                                              my
                                              legs
                                              out
                                              long.
Before I sleep I sing the same sweet song.

Oh   let   me   fly   like   Michael.

MOST PLAYERS DON'T GO PRO:

Most players don't go pro
most players don't go
most players don't
most players
most
most
must
must
must keep the books as open
as the   o p e n shot
inside   for the easy
lay up   for the easy
two.
In s i d e the books is just
the place   to go
after   the   final
whistle b l o w s.

A f t e r game and fame you
need to sign your
name on ch e c ks.
You
need tolive alife
s   t   r   o   n   g
into   the   next
g e n er a tion.

BEFORE MY MOTHER YELLS HER DINNER INVITATION:

even

before my father is ready to check my home
                                                                        work,

and   the television   explodes   the   house;

in

almost

darkness

I

can

b e

b o t h

c a t

and

mouse   moving   my feet   suddenly turning   my head.

                        I b l o c k   my own shot.

                        I s t e a l   my own   pass.

                        I s t a r   for both teams.

                        I   always   carry the b a l l

                            inside   to the table

                                        for the p o s t

                                                    game

                        in ter view s.

TABLE OF CONTENTS

SIMON & SCHUSTER BOOKS FOR YOUNG READERS
An imprint of Simon & Schuster Children's Publishing Division
1230 Avenue of the Americas, New York, New York 10020
Text copyright © 2000 by Arnold Adoff
Illustrations copyright © 2000 by Michael Weaver
All rights reserved including the right of reproduction in whole or in part in any form. SIMON & SCHUSTER BOOKS FOR YOUNG READERS is a trademark of Simon & Schuster.
Book design by Kristina Albertson
The text of this book is set in 11.5-point Gill Sans Bold. The illustrations are rendered in gouache on Crescent watercolor board.
Printed in Hong Kong
10 9 8 7 6 5 4 3 2 1
Library of Congress Cataloging-in-Publication Data

Adoff, Arnold.
The basket counts / by Arnold Adoff ; illustrated by Michael Weaver. — 1st ed.
p.   cm.
Summary: Illustrations and poetic text describe the movement and feel of the game of basketball.
ISBN 0-689-80108-4 (hardcover)
1. Basketball—Juvenile poetry. 2. Children's poetry, American. [1. Basketball—Poetry. 2. American poetry.] I. Weaver, Michael, 1962- ill. II. Title.
PS3551.D66B37 2000   811'.54—dc21   98-47941   CIP

first edition